W9-CDD-560

THE TIDE WON'T WAIT

THE TIDE WON'T WAIT

A Nova Scotia story told and pictured by LAURA BANNON

ALBERT WHITMAN & COMPANY • CHICAGO

Published simultaneously in The Dominion of Canada by George J. McLeod, Ltd., Toronto. Printed in the U.S.A. Library of Congress Card Number 57-6650.

My thanks to George E. Herman, chief of the Nova Scotia Travel Bureau, for his thoughtful assistance during my research for this story.

My thanks also to Mr. Russell Mack who owns the unique fishery at Minudie.

My gratitude to Mrs. Carlyle Pugsley who graciously took in a stranger during the busy haying season.

Laura Bannon

THE TIDE

THE TIDE was out when Worrell went to bed. The bare wet floor of the Nova Scotia bay gleamed in the moonlight.

While Worrell slept the great tide of Fundy surged back into the bay, bringing the shad fish. Salt water, thirty feet deep, filled the basin from dike to dike.

By the time Worrell woke in the morning the tide was racing out again, giving the shad a free ride back to the Bay of Fundy—except those that hung high and dry in Dad's nets.

Worrell rolled over in bed and blinked at the morning sun. His first thought was, "No school today. I can go along with Dad and Ted to clear the nets."

A screen door creaked. Worrell lifted his head, listening. Padded feet raced up the stairs. A loose, leathery face peeped around the door.

Worrell chuckled. "Hippo, you old rascal! You know you're not supposed to sneak into the house."

The big dog lunged at Worrell. The two tussled on the floor–quietly so Mom wouldn't hear them.

"Worrell!" That was Mom's voice calling up the stairs. "Worrell, get up. Breakfast's ready. And I have news for you."

Worrell dashed to the bathroom and splashed water on his face. He slicked back his hair with one quick swipe of a wet comb.

He knew that Grandfather, who lived in Truro, was sick and that Dad was driving there to see him after the nets were cleared. Could the news be about Grandfather?

Worrell dressed in a hurry and ran down the stairs with Hippo. "Quiet now," he warned. "If Mom catches you in the house you'll get what-for." He silently pushed open the screen door of the living room and let the dog slide out.

Dad and Worrell's big brother Ted

were already at the breakfast table. Mom was bringing in a platter of bacon and eggs.

"What's the news?" asked Worrell.

"You're going to have company," said Mom.

"Golly! Who?" A boy, he hoped. It would be fun to have a fellow his own age to do things with.

"Your Aunt Sally telephoned," Mom said. "She is on her way to Truro to see Grandfather. She brought Annabelle with her as far as Amherst and is putting

her on a bus to come down here. So you'll have your little cousin to play with for a few days."

"Play with Annabelle! Aw, Mom!" Worrell wrinkled up his freckled nose.

Ted grinned and said, "She must be quite grown up by now. You might enjoy her."

"Like a toothache," Worrell grumbled. "Once a sissy, always a sissy."

The last time Annabelle visited the farm she wasn't more than six, but Worrell remembered her only too well.

She always wore a ruffled dress. And she wouldn't do anything that mussed it or got it dirty. When she screamed like a wildcat for his toys he had to pass them over to her because she was so delicate. She always had an awful, drippy cold.

If Dad would let him go out to the nets, he could get away from her part of the time any way.

"Can I go with you to clear the nets this morning, Dad?" Worrell asked.

"Annabelle will be arriving before we get back," said Dad. "Do you think you should leave when you know she's coming?"

Worrell stared gloomily at his plate. The very thought of a visit from Annabelle spoiled his appetite.

Then he brightened. "You'll be gone tonight, Dad. Won't Ted need me to help him clear the nets tonight? I can go along then, can't I? Can't I, please?"

For just about his whole life Worrell had been wanting to go out on the flats in the pitch-dark night when they used the big battery light. Had the time come? Under the edge of the table, he crossed two fingers and waited for the answer.

"If the weather turns bad," Dad said, "Ted won't be going. It's too risky. The catch will just have to wait until the next low tide."

Worrell knew that if the nets weren't cleared at each low tide, much of the catch was lost. Shad will spoil when left hanging in the hot sun and they are often torn by the seagulls or are washed free by the next tide. Dad couldn't afford that.

"But the chances are we'll have a

clear moonlight night tonight," Dad added. "And if Ted goes, you can go with him. So cheer up."

Cheer spread all over Worrell's face. "I'll have more bacon and eggs, please," he said.

After breakfast Ted hitched up the horse while Dad and Worrell loaded

tubs into the box cart along with the pile of burlap that was used to keep the sun off the fish.

"How long will it be before Annabelle gets here?" asked Worrell.

"Worrell's getting anxious," Ted teased.

Anxious! He dreaded it. Every time

he thought about Annabelle, he had the same feeling he got when he swallowed too big a bite.

Dad looked at his watch and said, "She should be here in about a half-hour if the bus isn't late. You have time to drive the cows down to the lower pasture before she comes."

When Dad started to drive off, Hippo didn't know what to do. He wanted to

go along, but he wouldn't go without Worrell. He raced back and forth between the cart and his master.

"Come on, fellow," called Worrell. "We have to take the cows to pasture."

The cows were bunched at the barnyard gate. The minute Worrell lowered the bars they crowded out.

As usual, old Blackie swung out of line to snatch a few bites from the vegetable

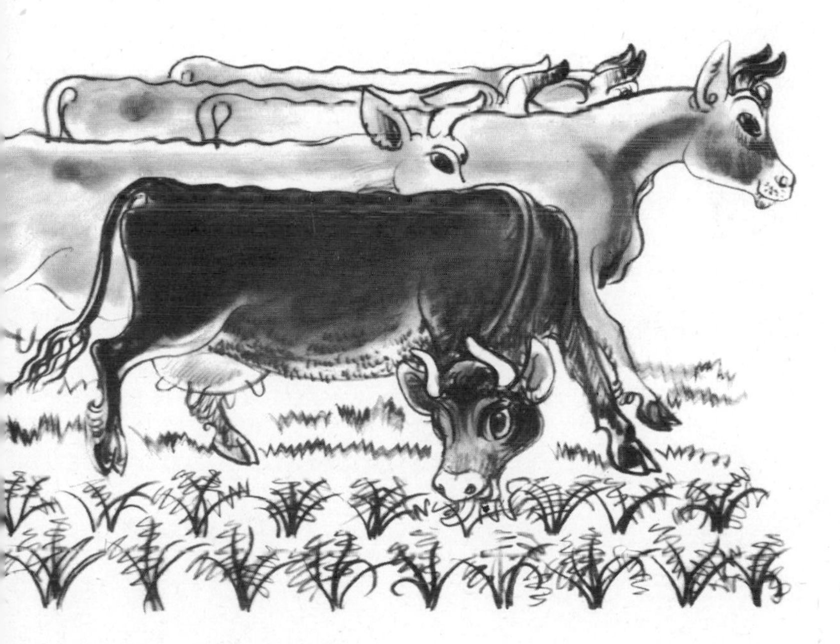

garden before Hippo could nip at her heels. But he soon had them all headed down the lane to the lower pasture.

"Annabelle will be surprised at Hippo's size," thought Worrell.

Hippo was only a puppy when she visited them before. Worrell would never forget the way she had mauled the little fellow. Well, one thing was sure. Nobody could mistreat Hippo now. He, Worrell, would see to that.

Worrell slowly closed the pasture gate behind the cows. On the way back he took the woodland path and looked for wild strawberries that had ripened since yesterday. No need to hurry.

"Anyway, Annabelle will be out of my hair when I go to clear the nets to-night," Worrell told himself. "She's too much of a sissy to want to go along."

Shrill, sharp yips came from the

direction of the house. Was that a dog? Worrell walked faster.

"Look! what's that under the apple tree?" he said to Hippo. "I don't know whether it's a dog or an overgrown caterpillar."

A small black-and-white fluff of fur bounced about under the tree. When it saw Hippo the yipping changed to a growl. The tiny dog rushed straight at the big one.

Hippo crouched behind Worrell's legs for protection. Worrell kicked at the little imp to keep him off.

A gale of laughter came from the leafy limbs of the tree. From below a branch, a pair of sneakers appeared.

A girl hung there by her hands. Then, as lightly as a leaf, she dropped to the ground.

"Hi, Worrell," she chirped.

"Hi, Annabelle," said Worrell.

"No one calls me that any more—

except Mother. I hate the name. Call me Ann, will you?"

Then Ann doubled over, laughing at the sight of the big dog cowering before the tiny one.

"That's a brave dog you have there, Worrell. And what a beauty! His face looks like an old satchel."

Worrell spoke up sharply. "He can be brave when it's necessary. Hippo doesn't like scrapping with caterpillars, that's all."

Ann laughed and caught up her small dog. "Quiet, Rowdy! You are scaring the life out of the big lummox."

She tilted her head back, still laughing, while her dog made passes at her chin with his tongue. "There's nothing cowardly about you, is there, Rowdy?" she said.

Worrell felt his ears burn. He grabbed Hippo's collar and led him to the woodshed. The big fellow was so nervous he was trembling. Yet at the same time he wagged his tail in apology.

Worrell stroked his pet to comfort him. To people who didn't know Hippo it was useless to explain how smart and brave he really was. He just didn't like to fight.

And so, if there wasn't a good reason for it, he didn't. Why should he?

Worrell was glad to hear Mom call, "I'm just taking cookies out of the oven. Would you two like some?"

Ann and Worrell perched on tall stools in the kitchen and ate warm sugar cookies. Rowdy, looking like a small penguin, sat on his haunches between them, begging for bites.

Ann wasn't bad to talk to when she stopped feeding Rowdy and paid attention to the conversation. You could almost like her when she just asked questions and listened to the answers.

She wanted to know all about going fishing with a horse, cart, and ladder. "How far is it out to the nets?" she asked.

"Oh, maybe as much as three miles," said Worrell.

"Is there any water at all in the bay when you drive out?"

Worrell crossed his legs and explained. "We usually start out when the tide is ebbing. There is still an inch or so of water. After it drains off, the tide slacks for about twenty minutes. Then in it comes again, faster than it went out."

"Do you have plenty of time to clear the nets and get back?"

"Man! There's no time to lose. We have to do a lot more than just gather the fish. Sometimes one of those tall poles is about to fall down. We have to swing it back and forth by its guy ropes until it sinks into the mud again. The nets have to be straightened too."

"Did you ever get caught by the tide?" Ann asked.

"Man alive! If I had, I wouldn't be sitting here. I'd have been sucked out into the Bay of Fundy in water thirty feet deep.

"But sometimes we have a hard time finding our way back to shore. Sometimes the fog rolls in so thick that a fellow can't tell time by his own watch. Gosh! The fog even gets so thick that the gulls have to walk."

Mom sat there keeping watch over a sheet of cookies in the oven. Worrell wished she wouldn't smile like that. But Ann was plenty impressed. You could tell. Her eyes had a new, shiny look—a look of really listening to something.

"How do you find your way home?" she asked.

"We follow a line of guide stakes," Worrell told her. "But sometimes they fall down and get covered by mud."

"Aren't you scared to go along?"

"Naw," said Worrell. "And I don't just go along. I help. I have to go tonight after dark to help Ted. After dark is when it's really dangerous."

Worrell was thinking, "After hearing all that, I bet she wouldn't go out on the flats for all the shad in the Atlantic."

"When do you go out again?" Ann wanted to know.

Worrell scowled, trying to figure the exact time. "Let's see. It's about six hours from high tide to low tide. And each tide comes in later than the one before it. So it's hard to figure."

He glanced at the clock. "Tonight we'll be leaving at . . . at about nine."

"I'm going, too," said Ann.

Worrell was so taken aback he could only stammer, "W-well, that's hardly possible. A girl shouldn't go out there at night."

Mom had been sitting with her head turned away, looking out the window. But now she joined in to say, "You know, dear, your mother wouldn't approve. Ted and Worrell won't return until long after your bed time. And, anyway, you'll see more if you go during the day."

Ann didn't answer. But as she left the kitchen with Worrell she said in a low voice, "We'll see about that later."

"She doesn't scream for what she wants any more," Worrell decided. "But I bet she's as set as cement about having her own way. Only this time I think she'll lose."

Ann was interested in everything alive in the big barn—the hungry new calves, the scary bull, and the twittering barn swallows. She watched the swallows wheel overhead, and she laughed when

they landed suddenly on the hay rope high in the gable.

"Jeeps!" she exclaimed. "They do that on purpose just for the fun of swinging."

Ann wanted to see the young lambs, tagging their mothers in the pasture. But Rowdy, who was always on hand, scared the sheep so they kept their distance.

"She's not a bad scout," Worrell decided. "Everything would be okay if she had left that pest of hers at home." If it weren't for Rowdy, Ann might even like Hippo. No one who really knew him could help liking him. But Worrell had to admit that Hippo wasn't at his best while moping under the porch.

When Hippo sneaked out and made a dash down the road, Ann laughed and called, "Watch yourself, Satchel-face, or you'll get scared by your own shadow."

"Hippo knows what he's doing," Worrell told her. "He knows Ted and Dad are coming. He always knows, long before we can see them over the top of the hill."

"I'll race you to meet them," Ann said. And she was off, keeping well in the lead. For a girl she was a pretty fast runner.

Worrell and Ann rode back to the fish shed with Dad and Ted and watched

them unload the tubs of fat shad. Then Dad left to get ready to go to Truro.

Ann asked a string of questions while she watched Ted salt down the catch. "Why do you slit the fish down the back instead of the belly? Why don't you cut off the head?"

Then suddenly she said, "Rowdy and

I are going with you tonight to clear the nets."

Ted only laughed at her. "Maybe if you are a good girl we'll take you along for a daytime trip when Dad gets back. But you'll have to leave that toy dog at home. A dogfish might snap him up."

Ann didn't seem to mind not being able to go. Worrell was beginning really to like her in spite of the way she made fun of Hippo. And he could tell that Ted liked her, too, by the way he kidded her along.

"Have you seen the bore yet?" Ted asked.

Ann lighted up like a struck match. "You have a boar around here! Is it savage?"

"It can be pretty wild at times," Ted told her. "Have Worrell show it to you."

"Show it to me now, Worrell, will you?

I've never seen a wild pig."

"Okay," said Worrell. "It usually runs along up the river at about this time. Maybe we can see it go past."

"Better leave Rowdy in the house," Ted warned. "Bores can do a lot of damage to small dogs."

"Will it attack people?" Ann asked.

"Oh, lots of people have been completely discombobulated by the bore," said Ted. "But you'll be safe if you don't go beyond the dike."

Ann shut Rowdy in the house and raced with Worrell across the barnyard.

They followed the brook past the yellow-green dike-land to a place where it ran through a wooden structure under the dike.

Ann paused to ask, "What's that?"

"It's an aboiteau," Worrell told her.

"That sounds more like a sneeze than the name of something." Just to prove it Ann made a first-class sneeze of the word when she asked, "What's an aboiteau?"

Worrell laughed. "There's a door under there that's hinged at the top. When the tide comes in, it pushes the door shut and keeps the salt water out of the dike-land. But when the tide is out, the water from the brook and the marsh ditches can run into the river."

Ann and Worrell were leaning over the bank, stretching their necks to see the door, when they heard Rowdy's shrill bark. He came bounding across the field straight into Ann's arms.

At that same moment Worrell whirled around and shouted, "I hear the bore. There it comes up the river and it is discombobulating. Run for your life!"

Ann was frantic. Clutching Rowdy, she tore after Worrell to the top of the dike.

The sound, like wind pushing through the trees, came nearer.

Worrell pointed. "Watch down the river."

A streak of white foam stretched across the basin from bank to bank. A

low wall of water came tumbling up the river.

Ann was not only excited. She was scared. "What's happening? Is it a flood?"

Worrell burst out laughing in spite of

himself. "That's the tide coming in. That's the bore." He spelled it for her. "B-o-r-e, not b-o-a-r."

"Oh, you!" Ann laughed with relief. "Well, I like the b-o-r-e better than any animal, except Rowdy. I love anything that has to do with water. Does the bore get bigger?"

"No," said Worrell. "The first push of the tide comes in fast enough to bank up that way. After that the bore moves on up the river and the water just rises."

They squatted on the dike and watched the river widen until it swallowed up a small island and crept up the banks of the dike.

"Let's get our swimming suits and take a dip," Ann suggested.

"The currents and whirlpools are dangerous when the tide is moving," Worrell told her. "I swim sometimes when the tide is slack and a grownup is along."

"I'm not afraid," Ann said. "I'm a good swimmer."

"It's a rule," said Worrell. "Kids by themselves don't swim down here."

Ann let the matter drop. Neither did she say anything more about going to clear the nets.

After lunch, while the sun was after-noon-hot, the two explored the cool woodland along the river. It was fun except that Rowdy drove all the wood creatures out of sight with his yipping.

Hippo never did that when he went with Worrell. For all his size he could be as quiet as a quail when they were out exploring.

After supper, while Worrell was busy with the chores, Ann became interested in a book.

Later in the evening she stood with the book under one arm and Rowdy in the other, watching Ted and Worrell load the fish tubs into the back of the cart. It was dusk when they drove up to the kitchen for supplies.

"Well, good night," Ann said. "See you in the morning. I'm going to read my book."

She disappeared in the direction of the guest room. But she popped her head back through the door to singsong a parting remark. "Now, Worrell, don't let the dogfish scare poor old Satchel-face."

Worrell, who was filling a sack with cookies, never looked up. "I just get to liking her, and then she has to say some-

thing like that," he told himself.

Soon afterward Ted, who had been keeping his eye on the clock, decided it was time to leave.

They had gone only a short distance when Worrell said, "What makes Hippo act so strangely?"

Hippo wasn't following each fresh track in his usual carefree way. He ran silently alongside the cart with his ears folded back.

"Come on, Hippo. Want to ride?" Worrell coaxed.

Ted stopped the cart, but Hippo refused to jump in.

"Our visitors must have put him in a bad mood," said Ted with a broad grin.

"Hippo wouldn't act that way without a reason," Worrell said.

When they pulled up in front of the fish shack, Hippo barked steadily.

"He wants to tell me something," Worrell decided. "What is it, old boy?"

Inside the shack Hippo stopped barking but he kept close to Worrell and watched the door. Ted built a fire in the sheet-iron stove and stood the teakettle on it.

Suddenly Hippo growled. At once someone knocked.

Ted opened the door. There stood Ann with Rowdy in her arms.

She laughed merrily and said, "May I warm myself by your fire?"

Rowdy snarled at Hippo, who slid under the cot where Worrell sat.

Ted asked soberly, "How did you get here, young lady?"

"In the back of the cart under that smelly burlap." Ann giggled. "I had such a time keeping Rowdy quiet. And I was afraid Hippo would give us away any minute. He knew we were there, of course."

"Well," now that you are here, you can keep the fire burning while we go out to clear the nets."

"After all the trouble I've gone to, getting here? I should say not! Don't be a stick-in-the-mud, Ted. Remember, I didn't get mad when you played that wild boar trick on me.

"This is not a joking matter," Ted told her seriously. "I won't be responsible. If you go, it will be without my permission."

Ann didn't answer. But Worrell could see that she was smothering her giggles.

She made Rowdy lie down and stop

barking. She brought cups from the cupboard for tea. Then, after Ted went outside to see how much the tide had ebbed, she burst out laughing.

"It was funny, Worrell. The fish smell

was gruesome under that burlap. I had to keep whispering to Rowdy to keep him quiet. And that talk about Hippo not liking the company! When all the time the company was listening!"

Ann giggled so hard that Worrell found himself laughing with her. But they sobered quickly when Ted returned.

"We can go out in about twenty minutes," he said. Then he turned to Ann. "Did you expect to go on the flats with only that light sweater to keep you warm? It's cold out there."

Ann struck a pose with hand on hip and chin high. "I always have my burlap wrap."

After drinking a cup of tea and eating four cookies, Ted gave up his grim manner. He found a heavy coat for Ann. And he didn't object when she climbed into the back of the cart with Worrell.

Rowdy's sharp nose peeped out from inside the old coat Ann wore. But disgruntled Hippo ran along under the cart.

A full moon climbed a sky ragged

with clouds.

Ted slapped the reins along the horse's flanks. "Come on, Jerry, walk up."

Jerry leaned into his harness and pulled the cart over the rounded dike and down the slope of gumbo, out onto the mud flats. He headed straight out, following the row of guide stakes.

As they left the shore, lights in the farmhouse windows blacked out, one by one. The world around them slept. The spongy mud of the empty flats smoth-ered all sound. Fog, caught in the big

battery light, streaked the velvet dark with silver.

Even Ann was quiet. She sat bolt upright, entranced.

Worrell told himself, "At last I'm out on the bottom of the bay in the dark night. And is it spooky!"

A train whistled over on the Canada mainland. A lone gull soared in a dark shadow across the sky, and screamed.

That loosened Ann's tongue. "Oh, I

wouldn't miss this for anything." Now she began asking more of her questions. "Why are the guide stakes set in such a crooked line?"

"If the stakes were set straight," Worrell told her, "they would look like one stake if you saw them from the end of the line. They could be missed at night or in a fog. But when they stand in a crooked line they make a big dark patch that shows up better."

"Let's get out and paddle along barefoot," Ann suggested.

"Oh, no, you don't," Ted spoke up sharply. "You stay put until we reach the nets. Then you can get out if you keep close to the cart. If you get lost out here, the tide won't wait until you are found. It would carry us all out to sea."

When they were near enough, Worrell pointed out the long string of billowing nets. At once Ann took off her sneakers and socks and rolled up her jeans.

As soon as they were close enough to see the silver-bellied fish, Ann and Rowdy raced ahead in the beam of light that Ted turned on them.

Ann pointed to the big fish, hanging by their gills, twelve feet above her head. "How did they ever get up there?" she shouted.

"I told you," Worrell shouted back.

"When the tide is in, the sea comes over the top of the nets."

"All that water!" Ann exclaimed. "This very day all kinds of fish were swimming around right here."

Worrell was used to the amazement of outsiders. They couldn't seem to realize that it was possible for the tide to fill the big bay and drain it again twice every twenty-five hours.

Ann jumped back into the cart with Worrell. Together they began to clear the lower half of the nets.

Somehow Ann's liveliness added to the excitement of being out on the flats in the dark of night.

"What's this ugly-looking thing?" Ann wanted to know.

She held up a blunt-nosed fish. It had a sour, turned-down mouth and a vicious spike in front of its dorsal fin.

"That's a dogfish," said Worrell. "They follow the shad to eat them."

"When all the time they would rather eat little dogs," Ann laughed. "Shall I put it with the other fish?"

"Throw it away," Worrell told her. "It's good for nothing. Not even sea gulls

will eat dogfish."

While Ann and Worrell cleared the lower part of each net, Ted cleared the top by using the ladder. He followed closely so that the light would serve them all.

It was a good catch. By the time the

fish were all in the tubs, the tide had turned and was coming in swiftly with the wind and a dense fog.

"A net is loose at the top of this pole," Ted called. "Hold the light for me, Worrell, while I fasten it. Then we'll be on our way to shore."

Ted climbed the ladder while Worrell trained the light on the top of the pole.

Just then Ann called out with alarm in her voice. "Here Rowdy! Come back, Rowdy."

Ted and Worrell turned to see Rowdy disappear into the fog with Ann after him.

"Ann, come back!" Ted shouted. "Let Rowdy go." He ran down the ladder at breakneck speed.

They heard Rowdy yelp. And then a muffled call, "Help!"

Ted grabbed the light from Worrell

and ran in the direction Ann had gone, combing the fog with the beam. But by now the fog was too thick to be pierced.

"Ann! Where are you?" screamed Ted.

They heard only the wind and water.

Hippo pressed close to Worrell, his ears back, his head down.

"Find her, Hippo," Worrell told him. "Go find Ann."

Hippo's tail went between his legs.

He understood all right. But he plainly didn't care a hang if the two visitors were lost on the flats to be swept to sea by the tide.

Worrell patted Hippo. Then pushing him and running with him, he commanded, "Come on! Come on! Find Ann."

Suddenly Hippo shot across the flats

toward the channel, just beyond the nets.

The channel is always dangerous. But when the tide comes flooding up the flats it is at its worst. Then the channel is a deep river of swift currents, whirlpools, and quicksands.

Worrell raced behind his dog. "Ted!" he yelled. "Ted! Over here! Turn the light this way. Hippo is finding her."

Ted located Hippo by his excited bark and fixed the light on him. Now he was at the edge of the channel. He was struggling to pull something out of the water.

Worrell watched in horror.

Ted reached into the channel and helped drag out Ann. She was clutching Rowdy.

"Are you all right?" Ted was saying.

"I think Rowdy is dead." Ann gulped and sobbed. "He fell into a whirlpool, and I went in after him. I couldn't get anywhere when I tried to swim. Oh, see if Rowdy is alive!"

Ted put the bedraggled mass of fur on his knee and tried to work the water out of the dog's lungs.

"I think he'll live," he told Ann.

Worrell gave his dry mackinaw to

Ann. She rode back to the fish shack, huddled in the seat beside Ted, sobbing and shivering and cuddling Rowdy. They stopped only long enough to get blankets, then urged Jerry on at his fastest pace.

Worrell rode in the back of the cart with Hippo. He rubbed him down with a piece of burlap and sat with his arms around his dog to keep him warm. No need to say anything. Hippo knew his

master was bursting with pride because he owned such a smart, brave dog.

Back home, an anxious Mom was waiting on the porch for them. She had missed Ann and was frantic with worry. She made her drink hot lemonade and go to bed under a stack of blankets.

Ann was still in bed the next morning when Worrell and Hippo slipped in to see her. Rowdy was wrapped in a towel by her side. He growled feebly at Hippo. But the big dog ignored him.

Ann was wearing a ruffled bed jacket of Mom's. Her eyes were red, and she was sniffling and sneezing into a handkerchief. Ann had an awful, drippy cold.

Hippo let her pat his head. In fact, he seemed to like it.

Ann's lower lip trembled when she said, "I don't know how to thank you,

Hippo. I laughed at you for being a coward and then you saved my life. I'm so ashamed."

"Aw, Hippo doesn't feel set up about it," said Worrell. "He's just naturally brave about things like that. Forget it, Annabelle."

That name just slipped out, but Ann didn't seem to mind.

Mom came into the room just then, and she didn't say one word against Hippo being in the house.